THE BEAR BOX

M. Luke McDonell

Thank you, Rusty, for traveling with me to Yosemite and everywhere else.

This story would not exist if not for feedback from the attendees of the amazing speculative fiction workshop led by Chris McKitterick, Director of the Ad Astra Center for Science Fiction & the Speculative Imagination at the University of Kansas.

Thanks to the Alabama Street Writer's Group for your thoughtful critiques and boundless support.

Thank you to all my friends who read this and gave feedback. I couldn't do this without you!

Anika's virtual coding room stuttered, flashes of the majestic natural beauty she'd been trying hard to ignore interrupting her work. Towering pines with puzzle-piece bark split parentheses and a clear blue sky erased the algorithms she'd scribbled across the ceiling. Resetting her glasses and cuff didn't fix the problem. Trees and sky remained.

"Dad. What's wrong? My glasses aren't working."

"I dunno, pumpkin. The pod's offline, too." Lights on the vehicle's dashboard screens pulsed red and he gripped the wheel with white-knuckled hands. Anika couldn't remember the last time she'd seen him drive manually.

Mom flipped the auto-drive switch off and on to no avail. "My glasses aren't working either. Maybe the rangers will know what's going on. Can you make it to the registration booth?"

Dad nodded and piloted them jerkily towards a small, peaked-roof brown gatehouse adjacent to the road. A chunky, asymmetrical wooden sign to the right read, "United States Department of the Interior, National Park Service, Yosemite National Park."

Anika's cuff chimed and a brown, jagged-tooth logo the same shape as the sign appeared on its screen. She poked it and scrolled through the menu.

Directions, Plan Your Visit, Eating & Sleeping, Things to Do, Calendar.

She looked for any external link, anything she could use to get onto WorldNet. Nothing. She was trapped in an endless Yosemite loop. She must be overlooking a poorly-designed

UI element. The WorldNet network literally spanned the globe.

Dad stopped abruptly by a window in the side of the gatehouse. A woman in an antique straw hat and buttoned-up gray shirt with a gold badge leaned out, morning sun winking on the metal.

"Welcome to Yosemite."

Anika was impressed that her cheery, outdoorsy smile didn't seem forced, though she'd have given it to hundreds of pods already today.

"Thanks," Dad said. "Is there some trouble with WorldNet? My pod is offline."

The ranger's smile did not falter. "You didn't read the orientation materials we sent."

"I did, we did," He looked at Mom, who shrugged. "I read most of it," he admitted.

"No problem," the ranger said. "I'll catch you up. There's no WorldNet connectivity in the valley, as per a National Park directive put in place on May first. We do have our own informational intranet, ValleyNet. There are kiosks in Yosemite Lodge you can use to make calls and send and receive messages to the outside world, but file size is limited."

No WorldNet? Impossible. Anika had never been without it. The green "connected" light, which she'd assumed was a permanent part of her cuff, glowed a sickly yellow. A wave of vertigo washed over her with the realization that the tether to everything important in her life had just been cut.

"What about the cats?" Mom said. "I have to lock the cat door after they're in for the night so the raccoons don't get in."

"I need to monitor the solar output," Dad said. "We're under producing and I'm not sure if it's cloud cover or something wrong with the inverters."

"I've got to work on my 3D modeling project this weekend." Anika's straight A record in high school was in danger of being broken by this one irritating class. If she didn't get full marks on the final she'd sink to a B+.

The ranger's smile fought a frown and lost. "We know this can be an inconvenience. That's why we had you sign a waiver."

"You knew about this, Dad?" Anika asked. He shook his head.

"Folks, I need to get you and everyone behind you checked in." The ranger indicated the growing line of pods behind theirs. "Let's start again. Welcome to Yosemite National Park. You're in for a treat. We had record-breaking amounts of snow this winter and the falls are spectacular. Sentinel bridge is closed for renovation, but everything else is open—at the moment. The river may reach flood stage later tonight which might affect low-lying areas of Housekeeping Camp."

"That's where we're staying." Dad handed the ranger the reservation form and she scanned the bar code.

"You'll be fine. Your cabin is on high ground near the store." She leaned out and stuck a plastic square onto the windshield. "You can turn on autopilot again. We have our own guidance system. It's about thirty miles to your cabin. Have a great time."

Mom switched on auto-drive and the dashboard lights changed to cheery green.

"Hang on," Anika said, "we're not going home?"

Mom shook her head. "Of course not. I'll go

to the lodge later and text Sheryl and ask her to check on the cats, and Dad can stop obsessing about the solar for a few days."

"I've got to work on my 3D modeling project," Anika insisted. "It's 50% of my grade. You promised I could."

"I did," Mom said, "and you can do whatever you can do offline."

"I can't do anything offline!" Anika didn't mean to wail, but her parents didn't grasp the seriousness of the situation. Not only could her GPA be affected, but without WorldNet she'd miss Chad's party Saturday night. Leanne was going to let her piggyback onto her glasses— which was almost better than being there in real life. Stealthy.

"Calm down," Mom said. "Your project isn't due for another two weeks."

"Riya, we did promise." Dad swiveled to face Anika. "Listen, pumpkin, I won't force you to stay, but this might be a once in a lifetime experience. It's a five-year wait just to get into the lottery for the chance to purchase tickets. Your mom and I have been trying every year since you were born."

Anika knew the story because her parents recited it at the slightest provocation. They'd come here when they'd first been dating. It was a magical, amazing place. So beautiful. Took their relationship from casual to serious. Blah, blah, blah.

"Sabine wants to see you," Mom added.

Anika groaned. She would play the Sabine card.

Mom and Dad had been bringing Anika on this annual Memorial Day weekend trip—a reunion with their U.C. Santa Cruz college roommates—every year of her life. Gabe, Alan, Sabine, and Dominic were more like aunts and uncles than her actual blood relatives. Sabine was her favorite, though. She treated Anika like a peer, despite their age difference.

"You've got to see Yosemite Falls before you decide. We'll stop there before we set up camp. It's great before noon. Rainbows," Dad said, waving his fingers in the air like a demented mime.

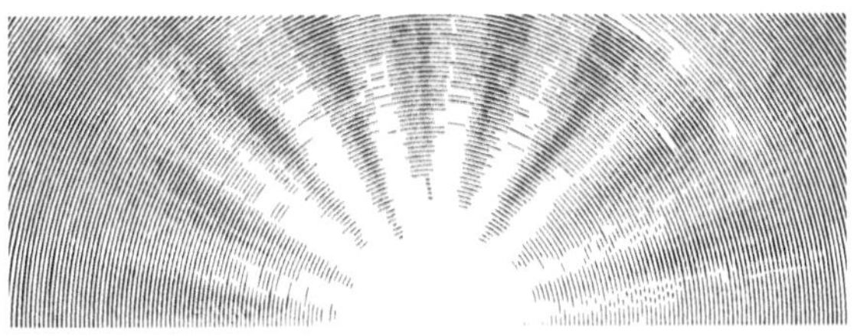

Anika stood on a timber bridge over a roiling green river, everything but her feet soaking wet and freezing cold, and stared upwards. Above her, rainbows, captives of the swirling mist, faded in and out of existence. The falls appeared behind them through ragged tears in the spray. More avalanche than water, a white plume cascaded over slick gray granite, crashing onto boulders far below.

The unevenness of the flow surprised her. From a distance it appeared uniform. Up close, the hundreds of streams contributing to the river didn't seem to have truly melded and plumes lived within the plume, some falling faster, some slower, some flinging themselves out into the air and never touching down, others angrily pounding the rocks that impeded their progress. The roar, too, changed its voice, the hiss and thunder a conversation in a language she didn't speak.

Many of Anika's favorite VR games took place in fantastical landscapes, so she should have been prepared for this scene, but the scale was beyond her comprehension and the resolution incredible. Something in her chest ached. She walked forward slowly, hands in front of her, expecting at any moment to run into a wall.

She knew the boundaries of her world. From the middle of her bedroom it was five steps to the desk. Two steps right to the closet. About face, and six paces to her bed. Reach left and touch the dresser. It wasn't much space, but she'd internalized it and could play nearly any game without running into anything.

She could walk a hundred miles here.

A blast of icy droplets hit her square in the face. She shivered. For now, walking back to the pod might be a good idea. She took one last look at the rainbows then dashed across the bridge and headed down the path.

The mist dissipated. Anika stripped off her sopping sweatshirt and tied it around her waist. The dry, fresh air was a welcome change from the damp San Francisco morning they'd left behind. Her parents strolled ahead, hand in hand, Mom's silver bangles jingling a pretty tune. Anika hadn't seen them hold hands in years. She slowed, letting the distance between them lengthen.

A family heading up the trail stopped and sent out a swarm of tiny drones to capture themselves and the distant falls from every angle. Anika considered following their lead. Her own GNAT was embedded in her cuff and should still work even without WorldNet, but what was the point? She couldn't send the images to anyone. Were her friends worried about her? She'd been offline for two hours now.

Birdsong replaced the fall's roar as the trail snaked downwards. A woodpecker landed on the specter of a lightning-struck tree and began hammering into the blackened bark. A squirrel raced across the asphalt, stopped, stood on its hind legs, then ran off. A lizard did push-ups on the low wall beside the trail and examined the world with swiveling eyes.

Anika smiled. The wildlife in her neighborhood consisted of pigeons pecking at a half-eaten hot dog or a rat flattened on the road. She took a deep breath of the pine-scented air and let it out slowly. She could leave right now. Grab a shared pod back to the Bay Area and work on her project and go to the party, or she could stay.

She consulted the lizard, still doing push-ups on the wall. He didn't have a strong opinion. Down, return to normal life. Up, see what other wonders Yosemite had to offer. Her cuff was no help either. For all she knew the party had been canceled and honestly, she needed a break from 3D modeling project and homework in general.

She took another deep breath and held it. She'd stay.

The lizard disappeared into a crack.

Housekeeping Camp was an eyesore. Anika wondered how the park service could have built something so ugly in the midst of such beauty. The pod crept slowly along the cracked asphalt street, passing poo-brown concrete block structures surrounded by barren dirt, fly-swarmed dumpsters, and so many parked pods and shuffling sunburnt tourists that if it weren't for the pines Anika would have sworn she was at a flea market in South City.

Even her parents seemed put off.

"I don't remember it being this crowded," Dad said.

"We didn't stay here," Mom said. "We camped in North Pines."

"It would have been nicer—" Dad started to say, but Mom laid a hand on his arm.

The pod—on autopilot since they'd left the falls—slid into a spot in a crowded parking lot adjacent to a sturdy log cabin sporting a rustically-carved "Registration" sign hanging in the eaves.

"Anika, check us in and find out where we're staying?" Mom offered the paper registration form.

Anika snatched it and got out. The camp smelled of dust and cooking meat. Her stomach rumbled. She hadn't eaten since breakfast and it was nearly noon. Hopefully Dad planned something good for lunch. He obsessed about the menus for these trips.

She clomped up the wooden-plank steps and held the squeaky screen door open for an exiting family, parents arguing in what sounded like Farsi, kids holding dripping orange popsicles, faces smeared with dirt and sugar.

The air inside was hot and still. Graphic posters of other national parks—Yellowstone, the Grand Canyon, Arches—lined the walls, the frames crudely secured with visible screws.

The couple in line in front of her, lanky Germans with overstuffed backpacks, moved aside. The young ranger behind the counter—unlike the buttoned-up professional at the front gate—seemed a bit undone. His wavy black hair might have been in a neat ponytail this morning, but it had since loosened, and a thick strand fell across his dark eyes. He pushed it back and it fell again. He was fit, muscular arms and shoulders hinting at, what? Swimming, maybe?

Anika and her friends weren't very athletic, so she couldn't identify the probable source of his physique. She prided herself on being attracted to brains, not bodies, but she considered making an exception for K. Sharma, as his name tag declared. The front pocket of his rumpled uniform shirt held a pencil and worn paper notebook. Anika hadn't seen a pencil in years, not since her sixth-grade teacher decided they needed to try drawing on paper. It had been a disaster, all the kids trying to "undo" their mistakes and failing.

"Welcome. You have a reservation?"

His voice was deep, but softer than she'd expected.

She slid the printout across the worn counter top.

He scanned the code. "You're in G-506. Just over there." He pointed through the wall to the left. The pencil came into play when he plucked a paper map from a pile and slashed a gray X through a square. "That's you. Showers are here. Bathrooms here." He X'd two other boxes.

"We don't have a bathroom in the cabin?"

"Nope. It isn't really a cabin. More like a roofed, semi-enclosed hut without a bathroom or power."

She glanced at his wrist, bare but for a smudge of what looked like chalk. She jangled her cuff. "These don't work here?"

He shook his head. "It's a new regulation.

A way to make sure that those who get the privilege of visiting here actually pay attention to what's around them. You heard about the man who drowned last month?"

She hadn't.

"He was playing 3D Scrabble—trying for a triple word score—and walked right off Sentinel Bridge. Hit his head on a rock, never surfaced."

"How do you know it was a triple word score? Maybe he was drawing a tile."

Anika hadn't meant to be funny, but the young ranger barked a laugh and looked her in the eye for the first time. His were hazel, ringed with darker brown, and she watched them change from bored to mischievous. He wasn't much older than she was; 19 or 20 at most.

"He was playing with the guy standing next to him. There was no reason either of them should have been in VR. There's a five-year waiting list just to get entered in the lottery."

The lottery thing made more sense now that she'd been to the falls. She could still hear their roar in the distance.

He returned to his rehearsed script. "Housekeeping Camp is the only place in the valley where campfires are permitted. You can buy wood next door. Fires need to be extinguished by 10 p.m. Food storage rules are simple but we do enforce them. You can keep food in your pod if you've got anti-theft protections, but whatever you take out must be locked in the bear boxes. Don't leave anything on the picnic tables or in the cabins. We've had several bear sightings in the past week."

"What do you mean, sightings? Aren't they in their pens?" Anika had paged through the Yosemite brochure on the way up and seen vids of a bear ambling past a split-rail fence.

Again, the ranger laughed. "The bears aren't locked up. They roam free. We do our best to preserve the valley in its natural state."

"That's insane! A bear can just walk up and attack me?"

"No one has been attacked by a bear in the valley in fifty years. If everyone keeps their food locked up, the bears will have no reason to come into camp."

The woman behind Anika interrupted.

"Can I please get my cabin number? I've got three kids in the pod and two of them have to pee."

Ranger K. Sharma's fingers brushed hers when he slid over the map. "I'm Kiaan. I'm giving a talk tonight at the Lower Pines Campground Amphitheater at 8:30 on the history of climbing in the valley. You should come."

A climber. That explained his arms.

"I will," Anika said, though she had no idea where Lower Pines Campground was, if she'd be allowed to go out, or if she'd want to chance it, given the bears. She exited through the squeaky door and headed back to the pod.

A woman grabbed Anika's arm and jerked her back. "Careful!"

A pod pulled into the parking place Anika was about to traverse.

"They can't see us," the woman explained. "The system here isn't very sophisticated. You've got to look both ways before you cross."

For real? Were they back in the stone age? Anika waited until the traffic cleared and made her way back to her parents.

Dad leaned out of the driver's-side window. "Well?"

"Hang on," Anika said, examining the paper map in confusion. It bore no resemblance to what she saw around her. Was that S-shaped squiggle supposed to be the road? In the Bay Area her glasses transposed a bright green line onto the sidewalk that she'd follow to her destination without thinking. Here they offered no guidance, so she'd stowed them. The low building to the left must be the bathrooms, so she used that, the road, and the X'd cabin to triangulate. G-506 should be just over there. She beckoned to the pod and Dad followed as she jogged ahead, then gestured to a battered beige fence with G-506 crudely painted on it.

"This is us!" she yelled.

A moment later Sabine emerged from behind the fence and enveloped Anika in a shaggy-haired hug. "You made it! Damn girl, you're even prettier than last year! How is that possible?"

A tall, pale, dishwater blonde with a red slash of lipstick, Sabine was the antithesis of Mom's compact, curvy frame, scrubbed-clean face, and smooth black hair. Sabine's husband Dominic, busy stringing up a hammock between two thin-trunked pines, waved.

"I've got news," Sabine continued once Dad and Mom had climbed out and claimed their hugs. "Gabe and Allan can't make it. Gabe's dad broke his hip this morning and they're flying to Phoenix to be with him."

"Why didn't Gabe message all of us?" Mom asked.

"He knew you'd be upset, and/or worried, and/or try to cancel the trip and he couldn't deal with any of that right now."

True enough. Mom was a problem solver even if the problems weren't hers or there was nothing she could do about them.

As Mom and Dad began to quietly argue about what this meant for the weekend, Sabine twined her arm around Anika's waist and steered her away.

"Gabe's dad is going to be fine. He's young. It wasn't one of those trip-and-fall things—it was a freak bike accident. They'll put in a pin and he'll make a full recovery."

Anika, a bit guiltily, realized she'd only been

concerned about the absence of the blowup couch Gabe usually brought.

"Gabe sold his camp vouchers to one of his coworkers," Sabine said, voice low, and glanced at G-508. "They've been bickering ever since they got here, and they've got a baby."

"Anika!" Dad called. "Can I get some help here?"

The oversized, solar-powered cooler he'd bought especially for this trip teetered precariously on the edge of the pod's hatchback. Anika ran over and grabbed a handle.

Together they lugged the gleaming silver box across camp and dropped it in front of a chest-high, rusted and filthy grayish brown container, its doors secured with multiple latches and chains. A sticker affixed to it screamed instructions in acid-yellow letters:

ALL FOOD MUST BE STORED IN THIS LOCKER.

Then in more reasonable black type:

LEAVE NO FOOD OUT. VIOLATORS WILL BE CITED. PROTECT YOSEMITE'S BEARS. REDUCE PROPERTY DAMAGE.

"Can you open it?" Dad asked.

Anika fumbled with the two latches, letting the chains fall with a clang, then struggled to loosen the metal crossbar. When the freed door fell forward, it let out a protracted shriek and groan and landed with a crash. A woman carrying a bag of groceries across the clearing grimaced.

They hoisted the cooler up and in, the bottom grating across pebbles and metal.

To the right of the bear box, a faded sign on the side of the cabin read:

WARNING. A BLACK BEAR HAS RECENTLY BEEN SEEN IN THIS AREA. DO NOT TO LEAVE SMALL CHILDREN UNATTENDED, CARRY A WALKING STICK, AND WAVE YOUR ARMS AND SHOUT IF A BEAR IS ENCOUNTERED.

Anika read the last part aloud. "Seriously Dad? I'm supposed to sleep here? There isn't even a door on this thing." Three sides of the cabin were concrete but the front was canvas, more a shower curtain than a protective barrier against predatory animals.

Dad ran his finger down the sign and it came away black with dust. "Don't worry. No one has been attacked by a bear here in decades. I checked. Now, get unpacked. Later this afternoon I'll to teach you how to build a fire."

Anika had never built a fire.

Fires weren't allowed in the zero-emissions zone of the Bay Area. She followed Dad's instructions and made a teepee of kindling over a crumpled mound of "This Week in Yosemite" newspapers. It felt horribly wrong to burn paper but a childish part of her grinned as she squirted lighter fluid over everything, struck a match, and exploded the pile into flames with a *woomph*.

"Whoa there, pyro!" Dad said. "We want coals for the burgers, not a conflagration. Wait until the kindling is really burning, then put on some bigger pieces. Make sure you've got good airflow. That's what keeps the fire going." He went back to the picnic table and continued slicing onions paper-thin the way Mom liked them.

Though Anika liked fire, she hated the

noxious, billowing smoke. Wherever she moved her chair, the smoke followed. As more fires were lit in the fire pits of Housekeeping Camp, more smoke rose, until the camp was smothered in a blue-gray haze.

The door flap of cabin G-508 fluttered and a woman carrying a white, fur clad bundle emerged. She approached, smiling shyly.

"I'm Charlotte. I work with Gabe. Do you mind?" She nodded towards an empty folding chair.

"Sure. I'm Anika."

The woman sat, patting the back of what Anika now realized was a baby dressed in a bunny outfit—puffy tail on butt, flapping ears on the hoodie. Anika was momentarily speechless. What idiot dressed their baby as actual bear food in Yosemite? Did this woman not see the huge warning sign on the bear box? It was readable even from here.

"My boyfriend forgot to bring chairs. We got the tickets from Gabe at the last minute and didn't have much time to prep."

Charlotte was as tall as Sabine but thinner, with an unexpected spray of freckles across her broad, pretty face. The greenish-yellow halo around one eye might have been avant-garde makeup, or maybe a healing bruise.

"What are you all doing for dinner?" Charlotte asked Anika.

"Hamburgers. Not sure what else. Gabe usually does side dishes and dessert."

The baby, face obscured by the oversized hoodie, drooled chunky white liquid onto Charlotte's striped t-shirt.

"Could we join you? I can make a salad."

Anika looked around for Dad. She didn't have the authority to make this decision. The baby—conveniently—chose this moment to transition from drool to fountain and Charlotte jumped up.

"Let me know. We're over there." She hurried back to the cabin.

No one was eager to have the mysterious couple to join them for dinner, but any excuse would have been pathetically transparent. Anika spread a red and white checked tablecloth over the picnic table, Mom set out ancient tin cups and plates, and Sabine whispered gossip. When Tad and Charlotte had arrived he'd gone straight to the store and didn't help Charlotte unload. He spent the afternoon downing a 12-pack of New Hamm's beer down by the river and threw the empty cans one by one into the fast-moving current. That last bit seemed to irritate Sabine more than his laziness and probable alcoholism. She worked for the EPA and that anyone would pollute this pristine water incensed her.

She and Mom gave Tad a good, long, side-eye when he emerged from the cabin, yawning, just as dinner was about to be served. He was a big guy, thick-necked like a football player, with small, close-set rat's eyes. The snake biotattoo on his arm swirled disconcertingly from bicep to wrist, over and over again. Anika hated tattoos like that but it gave her something to focus on when Tad shook her hand for way too long when Charlotte introduced her.

Dad grilled his famous burgers over Anika's perfect coals and Charlotte contributed a decent salad. The conversation wasn't what it could have been, thanks to Tad disagreeing with anything anyone said. Anika touched her cuff often, forgetting she was offline, intending to check in on Chad's party, see if her package arrived, make sure the cat was okay. It was disconcerting to find only dead gray when she glanced down.

The last of the sunlight crept up Half Dome, honey brightness sucked slowly into the darkening sky. She hadn't noticed the famous rock when they arrived, but it jumped out from between the pines in golden splendor as the sun set.

As the day expired, Housekeeping Camp came to life. Ugly cabins faded away. Campers who'd known about the lack of electricity brought solar-powered lights, and the rainbow-hued baubles gave the place the air of a carnival. Young kids fueled by too many roasted marshmallows ran by with low-power lasers flailing, beams of light casting crazed shadows. Laughing groups surrounded each campfire, faces reduced to orange and black masks by the flames.

Anika sniffed. Drifting above the bass thrum of wood smoke were the reedy notes of exhaled marijuana. She'd never tried it, thanks to her cuff, which until she was eighteen was the ultimate tattletale, sending her location and biometric data and a thousand other bytes back to her parents. That it was Sabine sucking on a red-tipped joint was no surprise. That she was skulking beside a dumpster was. Pot was legal for adults. Anika hoisted herself out of the rickety chair and crept into the shadows.

"Why are you hiding?" she asked.

Sabine pulled her around to the back side of the bin. "Tad. Charlotte told me he's on probation. He assaulted a coworker." She balled up her fist and waved the joint around like she was playing with a sparkler. "He's in anger management classes and isn't allowed to drink or do drugs. Normally his cuff would send an alert to his case manager if it detected alcohol in his bloodstream, but not this weekend thanks to Yosemite being offline."

Anika looked from the joint to her cuff—and the reality of where she was and what was possible rolled over her like an avalanche. The cuff wasn't just disconnected from WorldNet, it was disconnected from the database that kept a record of every step and breath she'd taken since she was born.

The status light on her cuff blinked impotent yellow, but to her they signaled green—Go.

"Can I try that?" she asked.

Sabine snorted. "Try it? You never have?"

Anika shook her head. "Not allowed."

"Your mom smoked pot in eighth grade. I don't know why she's being such a hard-ass with you."

"All the studies," Anika said. "She has data on how everything will affect my brain. Drugs. Pollution. Sugar. High altitude. Sex."

Sabine coughed. "Excuse me? Sex?

"Not sex exactly. It's about the age of consent. My mom is convinced that I shouldn't make any major life decisions until I'm eighteen. I can't even apply to colleges."

"You haven't had sex?"

Anika hadn't. Her virginity chafed like a two-sizes-too-small school uniform. California dropped the age of consent to sixteen a decade ago, but it remained at eighteen in her house. She wasn't sure if the cuff could tell, technically, when she did the deed, but it reported her biometric data, and the idea that her parents could sketch her sex life from the rising and falling lines sickened her.

"No. All my friends have. Or claim they have." She didn't mind sharing this with Sabine, who, based on the scowl on her face, was already climbing onto her sex-positive bandstand.

"Sex is a natural part of a healthy life. You're a smart, strong woman. I'd talk to your mom about it, but I promised I'd never give her any parenting advice, even when I think she's being crazy. In the meantime," Sabine offered the fat cigarette. "Have at it, girlfriend. Don't breathe too deep."

Anika breathed too deep, burned her

fingers, and dropped the joint. Sabine stomped out the small fire that ensued as Anika hacked.

"Damn, these pine needles are flammable. You okay?" She patted Anika's back.

"I'm fine," Anika croaked, trying to swallow away the rawness in her throat. Why would anyone intentionally smoke? It was awful, worse than what she'd been avoiding all night from the campfires. She checked the cuff. Still yellow.

"You feel anything?" Sabine asked.

Anika, lightheaded from the coughing, wasn't sure.

"Don't tell your mom, okay? I don't want a lecture."

Sabine rejoined the others around the fire; Anika snuck around the cabin to the public bathroom to wash out her mouth and give any lingering pot smoke time to dissipate.

Was she stoned? She wanted to be so she could talk about it casually the way her friends did. She stared into the bathroom mirror, face too brightly lit by the white glow-ceiling. Her eyes were bloodshot, but she hadn't worn glasses all day and the Sierra sun had been intense. Her carefully straightened dark brown hair was wavy and wild from the wetness of the falls and her eyeliner smudged in a "just woken up" way that would have taken a makeup artist an hour to craft. She looked good. That made her giggle. A little girl in unicorn pajamas—brushing her teeth at the next sink over—looked up quizzically.

"I'm okay," Anika said, and the little girl nodded solemnly, the foam around her mouth giving her the look of a rabid squirrel.

Once she was back outside, Anika caught fragments of conversations as she took the long way back to the cabin. The adult campers, animated by the beers they brandished, drove home Very Important Points about sea surface temperature, earthquakes in Yellowstone, the great fish die-off, and other WorldNet topics.

She returned to find her own campfire ignited by the same spirits.

Tad held a liter bottle of tequila, Dad, a flask of some of the awful "artisanal" vodka he'd distilled in their garage.

"Things are much better now," Dad said. "Do you know what the per capita murder rate was in 2020?"

He fumbled for his glasses to search for the data. Anika smiled. He loved supporting his opinions with facts—and there was a fact for just about any opinion. She'd learned that years ago, but didn't trot out her own data anymore. Any argument she won sent him scrambling until the dinner table was a battleground littered with statistics and uneaten turkey meatloaf. Mom finally banned glasses at mealtime.

Dad covered his habitual but now useless gesture—glasses wouldn't work when the cuff was offline—by smoothing back his hair.

"It was high," he continued. "Really high. The crime rate is half what it used to be. Plus, the U.S. incarcerated more people than any other country on the planet. Now we're near the bottom of that list."

"You know what other list we're at the bottom of?" Tad asked, voice slurred. The too-tight collar of his white t-shirt strained against his thick neck. "Innovation. We used to be number one. We used to break the rules. Startups used to have fridges full of beer and everyone smoked pot and did blow and came up with crazy ideas and got money to develop those ideas and then worked too hard and stayed up too late. Sure, a lot of the companies tanked, but we got some amazing products. Too bad one of them was this."

He held up the oversized bottle of tequila and Anika was confused for a moment until she realized he meant the cuff on his wrist.

"Now we live in self-imposed prisons. I can't work past six p.m. This fucking thing shuts me down to help manage my 'work/life' balance. Makes sure I take time to be a good father." He spat out the last word out. "God forbid my blood sugar level drops or my heart beats too fast for too long—"

The baby, who'd been emitting half-hearted squawks, hiccuped then let out an ear-piercing wail. Anika winced. The sound would have inspired dogs to howl if any had been near.

Tad spun, his boots kicking up dust. "I told you to keep him quiet," he growled.

"He didn't get his nap," Charlotte whispered when the baby paused to suck in a breath. Maybe she was trying to average out the volume. "I'll take him for a walk."

She disappeared into the night, the wails fading like the distant sirens Anika heard from her bedroom every night.

"Where was I?" Tad asked, then belched.

Anika pulled a chair away from the fire and slumped into it, tuning him and the ensuing tech argument, out. She'd heard variations on this theme at the dinner table for years. Dad was in favor of the cuff, while Mom weakly supported less monitoring, though not for her own daughter of course.

The discussion bored her because the deal was done. Employees, students, family members, each signed on for a different reason, but at the end of the day, they all wore cuffs. She'd worn one since birth. Once she was sixteen no law required it, but it stored her music and images, health records, transit pass, credits, contacts, and managed her WorldNet access. Life would be a pain in the ass without it. She got the latest model every year on her birthday. This one shimmered like a mermaid's tail, each iridescent scale a high-def screen with real-world resolution, but her conduit to the world was also a leash.

Except for now. It was untethered to arbitrary rules. She leaned back and imagined her friend Leanne's face when she told her she got stoned. *Finally*, she'd say, but she'd be impressed.

The adults yammered and the sky slowly deepened from cerulean to deep blue, the trees a black fringe against it. The first star shone bright. The argument had petered out and Mom, Dad, Sabine, and Dominic roasted marshmallows, laughing when one caught fire. Tad lay horizontal in Dad's lounger, mouth open, snoring. Charlotte paced the perimeter of the firelight, jiggling the baby in the rabbit outfit.

Shit. What time was it? Kiaan's talk was at 8:30. Anika stood and could just make out a plastic clock on the side of the bathroom. 8:15. Would she make it in time?

"I'm going to a ranger talk," Anika announced.

"Sounds good," Dad said, wiping sticky white from his chin. "Be back before midnight?"

"Way before."

Anika grabbed her backpack and unfolded the Yosemite map. She'd never navigated by an old-fashioned map before today. Lower Pines Campground was across the river and to the right. As she headed out of the glow of the firelight she stumbled over something. Not the beer bottle she'd expected, but a nearly-empty liter bottle of tequila. She picked it up, expecting one of the marshmallow-roasters to admonish her, but when none did she jammed it into her pack. Tad wasn't supposed to be drinking so she was doing the world a favor.

Anika followed a parade of young LED-holders and their parents towards the amphitheater, figuring there was safety in numbers if any bears were around. Once they'd crossed the bridge and the amphitheater was in sight, floodlights beaming, she slunk off the path and into the shadow of a large pine.

She took out the tequila, pulled the cork and sniffed. The rotten sweet sharp scent nauseated her, but she took a sip anyway. Her tongue burned. The fire soon faded to warmth. Kids passed by, not seeing her in the darkness. She took another sip. Not quite as bad this time. The warmth in her mouth slid down her throat, into her stomach, and out to her limbs, dispelling a tension she didn't know she'd been holding.

The lights of the amphitheater brightened and the crowd quieted. Anika re-corked the bottle, nestled it in the pack, and snuck onto a log bench in the back row. The theater was little more than a wooden backdrop surrounded by a semi-circle of tiered benches. She applauded enthusiastically when Kiaan stepped onto the low stage. He was still in uniform, though maybe a fresh one, and he'd gotten his hair under control.

"In 1869, John Muir made his first ascent of Cathedral Peak," he began, and continued with a long list of Muir's other firsts.

Anika's leg began to jiggle of its own accord. As attractive as Kiaan was under the glow of the LEDs—and he was better looking than any guy in her class—it was hard sitting through a history lesson. This was supposed to be vacation.

Then, magically, a white stub of granite rose from the stage floor. Kiaan stepped aside as it thrust higher than the backdrop.

The audience, as one, drew in a breath, then laughed, everyone realizing at once that a state-of-the-art holoprojector was hidden somewhere amongst the rustic furniture.

The presentation picked up after that.

Kiaan padded around stunning recreations of Cathedral Peak, El Capitan, Half Dome, Lost Arrow Spire, and others, giving names and personalities to formations she'd mistakenly assumed were anonymous rocks. He populated these with the men, and later women, who had climbed them, their routes crooked bright green lines transposed onto impossibly sheer faces. He moved as gracefully as a dancer as he manipulated the 3D images—reaching, pushing and pulling, zooming in from 10,000 feet to a close view of climbers huddled on a Portaledge during a storm.

Everything about climbing looked terrifying to Anika, but Kiaan clearly loved it, his smile growing wide as he pantomimed working his fingers into a crack or rappelling down a wall of granite after successfully reaching the summit.

The 45-minute talk ended too soon. As the projection faded and the lights brightened, Kiaan invited anyone who was interested to stay for a brief discussion of bouldering, his new passion.

Anika worked her way forward against the tide of departing families. She wasn't interested bouldering. She'd never heard the term before tonight. She was, however, interested in Kiaan.

A small crowd surrounded him, most of them climbers she guessed from their physiques. She sat on a bench in the front row almost out of earshot and heard only snippets—Camp Four, Midnight Lightning, chipping—none of which meant anything to her, but she enjoyed Kiaan's eagerness, his easy familiarity with strangers who shared his passion. She slid closer.

"It's climbing stripped down. No ropes. No harnesses. Nothing but me, my shoes, my skills, my problem-solving abilities. Nothing between me and the rock," he enthused, tucking that same strand of hair behind his ear that had fallen loose at the registration desk.

Anika sat up straight. A wonderful, awful idea slipped into her mind like a piton into a crack, and lodged firm. Was this her chance? She'd had many firsts tonight. First hit off a joint, first sips of alcohol…could she tackle the big one?

She'd gotten straight A's in calculus and most of her other STEM classes. Virginity was the only problem she'd been unable to solve.

It wouldn't hurt to try. But how? Though she'd researched the sex act as thoroughly as a clinician, studying the ins and outs in VR, she'd neglected any study of seduction. If anything, she'd perfected the opposite—the art of saying no. She'd gotten the best of both worlds from her parents—Dad's height and Mom's curves and sharp intelligence—and because of this she and the cuff had been successfully fending off sexual advances since she was 13. Could she persuade Kiaan, and herself, to say yes?

He caught sight of her, and his smile broadened. He held up a finger to signal one moment.

The spotlights around the theater winked out one by one until only the glowlights above the backdrop remained. The climbers, taking their cue, shook Kiaan's hand or slapped him on the back, then shouldered their packs and headed out.

Kiaan sat down next to her. "G-506. You came."

"Anika," she said.

"What did you think?"

"It was great. You were great."

"Really?" He'd looked older and taller on stage, but now, with puppy-dog yearning for approval in his mahogany eyes, he could have been any of her guy friends.

"You actually climb the mountains you showed us tonight?"

He waggled his hand back and forth. "A few of them. I'm more into bouldering now. It's nice because you don't need much gear. Just shoes and chalk. And you don't damage the rock with pitons and bolts."

"Sounds scary."

"Not scary." He turned towards her, hands springing into motion again. "Challenging. The climbs I showed tonight followed routes. In bouldering we call those 'problems.' Each boulder is a problem you solve with your body *and* your mind."

Anika laughed. "We pretty much only solve mind problems at my school."

"They're doing you a disservice. I've been trying to get the park to let me give bouldering classes, but there are liability issues. I could give you a demonstration though, on Monday—if you're still here?"

"Yes, that would be great." She clutched the backpack to her chest, looked into his eyes, looked away. What was she supposed to do next? "I'm not sure how to get back to Housekeeping Camp," was all she could muster. "I'm not very good at maps."

He nodded. "It's a common problem. I can walk you back. Let me close this place down and get my bag."

He disappeared behind the stage and a moment later the backdrop lights faded until she was alone in the gloom. The moon might have provided illumination, but it hung low, obscured by trees. In the city, darkness was a choice, and one that was hard to make. Even with eyes closed at night she could see ghosts of streetlights, charging lights, and screens drifting on her bedroom walls. Here, there was no choice. Darkness…was.

She squeaked when Kiaan materialized beside her.

"Sorry." He turned on a flashlight and the world shrank to the size of the blue white circle that enclosed them. "You want to take the scenic route? Half Dome looks amazing when the moon's full."

"Sure."

Was this Kiaan trying to get her alone or

Ranger K. Sharma enthusing about the rocks he loved? She followed him out of the circle of benches and down a dirt path into the woods. After she'd stumbled twice, he took her hand. His was, as she'd expected, warm and calloused. She hoped hers wasn't sweaty.

"It might be better if we turn off the flashlight and let our eyes adjust," he said.

"What about the bears?" Every boulder and fallen tree they passed had claws and flashing eyes.

"We'd be lucky to spot one. We don't see many on the valley floor anymore. With the huge number of visitors…" He paused, perhaps realizing Anika was one of the large number of visitors screwing up the ecosystem. "Anyway, no one has been attacked by a bear in decades. They'd rather eat berries than us."

He pulled her forward and the landscape slowly transformed from dead black to shifting grays and blues. Her heart beat with the same giddy fear she'd felt riding down a too-steep hill on a hoverboard. She wasn't frightened of Kiaan—who held her hand with professional courtesy and kept his eyes on the path—but of her own intentions. She took a deep breath. Nothing was inevitable, not yet.

The trees fell away and they emerged into an almost daylight-bright meadow. Kiaan stopped abruptly. When she bumped against him, he was soft and solid at the same time and smelled the way she wished campfires did. Smokey like sandalwood and maple syrup.

Half Dome, an obsidian absence of stars, towered above them. The river, which she hadn't realized was so near, ran wide and deep and silent. Strange eddies caught the moonlight and the inky water undulated and swirled languidly.

Kiaan puffed out a breath. "It'll look better an hour from now. The moon is going to rise just above the peak. Can you wait?"

"Sure."

He led her to a flat bench of a rock near the river and they sat, thighs touching.

Neither of them needed to fill the silence because there wasn't any. Subtle, unfamiliar sounds filled the spring night. No blaring sirens, drone fights, dogs barking, next-door neighbors playing hologames in their backyard. The pines whispered secrets to each other in the faint breeze. Something small, a mouse perhaps, rustled in the dry leaves. The river wasn't as silent as she'd first thought, its murmuring not quite coinciding with the swells and depressions dappling its surface.

Kiaan studied the sky. In the dimness, chin lifted, he looked like something from art history. A Greek or Roman sculpture. Strong, smooth—archetypal. The guys in her class were bad sketches of teenage awkwardness and angst.

She took a deep breath and shifted a hand from her lap to his knee.

His attention snapped from the heavens to her. After a moment's hesitation, he stroked her cheek with the back of his hand, then leaned in for a kiss. It was a good one. The kisses she'd shared until now had been more eager than practiced. Kiaan had it just right.

A few minutes later, they began to teeter towards the horizontal, Anika surprised to find herself the aggressor.

"Hang on a sec," Kiaan said. "I've got a place we can be more comfortable."

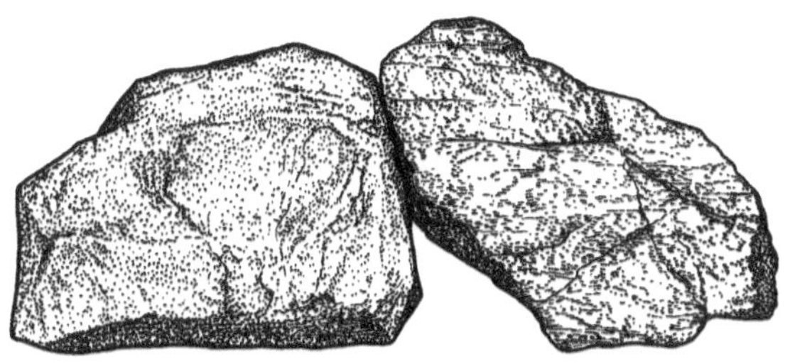

He did—and it was an actual, literal, cave. Three truck-sized granite boulders on the far side of the meadow nestled against each other to create an A-frame space. Anika froze when the flashlight revealed a mattress on the ground. She didn't mind him being more experienced, but this was a bit much.

"That's my crash pad," he explained. "For bouldering. So I don't hurt myself when I fall. I climb here." He raised the light to a pair of dusty shoes hanging from a tree limb wedged between the rocks.

Anika didn't relax much. She was in the middle of the wilderness with a stranger. A polite stranger who didn't seem like he was about to murder her, but was this a good idea? Her cuff hung limply on her wrist, obstinately silent.

Kiaan dimmed the flashlight and set it into one of the shoes. It swung gently, the mica in the granite winking in the diffuse light.

"Do you mind?" he asked as he unbuttoned his shirt. "I don't want to wrinkle this. I've got to wear it tomorrow."

His offhandedness disturbed her. She stood on the threshold, one foot in the cave, the other inching towards the river. Now that her eyes were adjusted to the darkness she could follow it back to the bridge, back to camp.

He hung his shirt carefully on the branch then turned to face her. The slash of scar on his tanned chest startled her from indecision.

"What happened?"

He ran his fingers down the raised red line, smiling ruefully. "I fell. I did land on the pad but there was a lot of rock between it and me." He turned to show his back. Four tears like he'd been mauled by a bear ran from his right shoulder to his lower back, these not fully healed. "Those are from last week. I fall pretty often. Bouldering is risky, but you can't improve without making mistakes."

When he held out his hand, she hesitated,

then took it, and they descended carefully to the mattress and continued what they'd begun by the river. Clothes fell away or were wriggled out of until they were skin to skin. Kiaan was, if anything, too much the instructor, telling her where to put her hands like she was a student in the bouldering lessons he wished he could give. To be fair, he also asked if he was getting it right. Were they going to "do it" or spend the night planning their route?

Unfortunately, when the big moment finally came, she'd giggled. After solemnly asking for her consent, Kiaan sprayed on a condom. It looked like bathroom cleaner as it bubbled and settled. In legal porn—where the actors had to wear condoms—they appeared as a rainbow sheen. She should have bought a can to see how it really worked.

Sex wasn't as uncomfortable as her drama-queen friend Leanne promised it would be, and neither was it as amazing as braggart Navya claimed. Anika held onto Kiaan and tried to keep her head from knocking against the granite. She envied his easy pleasure, but knew from everything she'd read that it would get better for her once she figured out what she liked. Indeed, once she was sure there were no more surprises ahead, she relaxed, and for a few moments she was with him, moving in time to an inaudible, quickening beat. The rock poking her right shoulder no longer bothered her, the mattress didn't smell of stale sweat, and the river stopped murmuring and listened. *Could it always be like this?* she wondered.

Some indeterminate time later, as Kiaan lay beside her, stroking her hair, murmuring compliments and fighting sleep, an unearthly shriek and groan cut into the cave from the darkness beyond. Anika tensed.

"Bear box," Kiaan whispered, "Don't worry." He pulled her closer.

The next shriek, a few minutes later, wasn't from a bear box. They both froze. A woman screamed, a long keening wail. The radio clipped to Kiaan's pack spat static.

"All rangers report to Housekeeping Camp. We have Code Adam. Repeat, Code Adam."

Kiaan leapt up and had his pants on before Anika could draw a startled breath.

"What does that mean?" she asked.

"Missing child," he said, pulling on his shirt. "I need to join the search party."

She scrambled for her own clothes.

"Sorry about this. I've got to run." He leaned down and kissed her, getting more chin than mouth in his haste. "Kids get lost every night here. They head to the bathroom, get disoriented, end up in the wrong cabin, and everyone panics. The more of us who show up to help, the faster we find them." He pointed towards the river. "There's a paved path just below where we were sitting earlier. Go right, and you'll end up at the bridge. You can't miss it. I'll check in with you at your cabin when I'm done."

Anika sat, dazed, holding her tank top to her chest as he loped off. What the hell? She hadn't imagined this de-virginizing scenario ending with her lover throwing on a uniform, running off to rescue a child, and leaving her alone in the wilderness. Should she feel hurt and abandoned?

Honestly, she was relieved. The missing child saved her from another uncomfortable first—the first exit. As Kiaan dozed, her arm trapped beneath him, she'd worried about the time, if she smelled like sex, where the showers were, how to dry off without a towel, and what to do if he asked for her contact info.

She hadn't planned to give it to him. Right now he was air-gapped from her real life, disconnected from WorldNet and hidden behind a mountain range.

She ventured a smile as she worked on her hiking boots. She'd done it. She was no longer a virgin and her cuff was none the wiser. She owned this data point. No rumors would reach her parents and she may or may not tell her judge-y friends. Having a private life for the first time in her life felt pretty good.

The moon was high when Anika emerged from the cave. Half Dome dominated the skyline, etched in the sharp relief Kiaan promised. What time was it? Her cuff could at least tell her that. Only 11. So much had happened in two and a half hours. She took a deep breath of the warm air. Did she feel different? A bit sore and a bit disappointed that passing from one state to another was like crossing actual state lines—no actual line, no change in scenery. Before Kiaan, she'd done "everything but" and somehow thought she wasn't having sex because Mom decreed sex was intercourse. She could see now what an arbitrary marker that was.

The paved path was easy to find now that the shadows of the trees had receded. The beam of the flashlight danced as she jogged to the bridge. She slowed to a walk to cross, pausing at its apex. Moonlight hit the river, shattered, and the pieces floated serenely towards Yosemite Falls, so distant it was nothing more than a silent, chalky scribble. The water level of the river was higher than it had been earlier, almost to the top of the lower piers, and she recalled the ranger mentioned potential flooding.

The river carried other passengers besides

the moonlight. A beer bottle. A neon-green tennis shoe. A tree trunk with gnarled roots. In the distance, something white bobbed then disappeared. Maybe a Styrofoam cooler. Maybe snow from a drift a thousand feet upstream.

The hiking boots chafed as she made her way back to Housekeeping Camp. She hadn't broken them in. Her plan to slip unobtrusively into the cabin vanished—given it was surrounded by a maelstrom of lights and agitated people. What was going on?

Mom ran over and crushed her in a hug. "Where were you?"

Over her shoulder, Anika saw an older ranger talking to Charlotte, who choked out words between sobs. Tad stood beside her, glowering and red-eyed in a brown, ratty bathrobe. The bear box lay open, leftovers from dinner scattered on the ground around it.

"I was at the ranger talk. What happened?" Anika asked.

Mom released her from the hug, but kept hold of her hand. "The baby's gone," she said. "He was in a crib in the tent cabin and when

Charlotte woke up to feed him, he wasn't there."

A woman near them spoke low and urgently to another ranger. "I saw something. I think it was a bear. Right there." She pointed to the clearing between the cabins where the embers from the fire still glowed. "It was big, kind of shuffling along." Her voice was calm but her eyes were wild, and a child, maybe 10 years old, held her hand in a death grip.

"Valley bears don't typically walk like that," the ranger said. "They stand to take a look around, then go back to all fours."

"Are you kidding?" Anika asked Mom. "Gone?"

"I'm not kidding. I'm going to get changed and help search."

Anika belatedly noticed Mom wore purple striped pajamas. Sabine, already dressed and ready to go, conferred with a ranger holding a glowing tablet.

"There's a baby-eating bear walking around here and you're going to look for it?"

Mom's smile was grim. "When you have kids of your own you'll understand." She disappeared into the cabin.

Anika, shivering in the nearly midnight chill, went to look for Dad. He stood under a bug-swarmed streetlight next to their parked pod, arguing with a ranger.

"Turn off whatever it is you use to block WorldNet. That baby has a cuff. We can find him," Dad said, his normally calm voice edging towards anger.

The woman nodded as she swiped through pages and poked check boxes on a ruggedized screen. "We're in the process of doing that. Unfortunately, this is hardware, not software, and there is no universal off switch. I've sent rangers to all the towers and they're powering them down."

She glanced up and Anika realized the silver balls on slender poles weren't lights, but something else.

"Every minute—" Dad started to say.

The ranger cut him off with a glare. "We know. We also know that Yosemite black bears don't sneak into tent cabins and quietly steal babies out of cribs. The Park Police are on their way and we're searching all pods leaving the valley."

Anika grabbed Dad's hand. "What happened to the baby?"

"I dunno, pumpkin." He dropped her hand and went back to arguing with the ranger.

She half-listened as aches in her body began to surface. She massaged her back, likely bruised by the rock under the too-thin mattress. Her head had hit granite when Kiaan had gotten a bit too enthusiastic near the end. When she rubbed the bump, her finger came away red. Her stomach churned and she worried she'd lose her dinner right then and there on the asphalt.

"It's not safe here, Dad. I want to go home," she said.

Dad didn't argue. "Put the pod in *Panic* mode and set it to loop the valley. We'll all leave once things are under control here."

Anika palmed the pod door, crawled into the back seat, and set the destination as infinite scenic loop. The dashboard claimed the interior temperature was 86 degrees but it felt like she was back at that awful immersive play Solanna dragged her to at midnight last December at Ocean Beach.

The pod circled the valley counterclockwise and Anika caught glimpses of strange tableaus in staccato flashes. Beams of light on tree trunks. Confused faces inside stopped pods. The river, overfilling its banks and slowly drowning a meadow. Mariposa County sheriffs knocking on doors of the Valley Lodge. Sniffer robots circling dumpsters. A fleet of drones passing overhead like bats.

She hated this place. What did they expect would happen when they put babies and bears together in a valley and made cabins without doors? Cabins that might be inundated by the river. Bridges with railings so low you could fall over them and drown. And the waterfalls—tons and tons of water smashing down without even a fence to protect people, just a sign warning the rocks were slippery. That was the understatement of the year. The squirrels and lizards probably carried Bubonic plague. There were a hundred ways to get hurt here—why not go ahead and disable the cuffs to make extra sure the worst could happen?

She closed her eyes and tried to breathe slowly and quiet her heart. She wanted to leave this place and never come back.

After eight trips around the park her cuff activated for a moment, then went back to standby mode. The next time around it stayed on for a few minutes. A long list of messages from friends snaked around her wrist. The subject lines should have been lifelines, but they only made her more nauseous. *Party pix from tonight. Jon called me fat. Red okay with these shoes? Hair emergency! Calistoga on Monday? Which kind of pasta are you?*

She pressed *Off* and the text vanished. What was she supposed to say? *Red looks great and, hey, there's a baby missing here that was either abducted or eaten by a bear.*

She tried to sleep but the transition from bright to dark as the pod passed under the irregularly-placed streetlights jarred her awake. That Dad hadn't called back the pod meant the baby hadn't been found, but the park was huge and searching every cabin in housekeeping camp would take hours. Fatigue finally drew her into a fitful sleep, and she dreamt of warning signs, shapes in the dark, and water covering her as a weight pressed her down.

Anika woke, groggily, when the pod lurched to a stop. She sat up and scrubbed at her chapped lips. Early morning sunlight filtered through the pines onto the dusty ground of Housekeeping Camp. The hatchback popped open, cool air rolled in, and the pod shifted when Dad dumped the cooler into the back.

"What's happening?" she asked.

"Nothing much," he said, though the tightness in his voice hinted that something was.

Over his shoulder, she saw Tad being maneuvered into the back seat of a Mariposa sheriff's pod. He wasn't handcuffed, but the

Park Service policewoman assisting him held a stunner, slightly raised, her finger on the trigger.

"Did they find the baby?" Anika whispered.

"They did not." Dad threw the bin with pots and pans on top of the cooler with too much force.

"Is Tad being arrested?"

The sheriff pod pulled away. Sabine hugged Charlotte as Dominic loaded gear into Charlotte's pod.

"Nope. They're taking him in for questioning. You heard him," Dad said. "We all did. He made 'father' sound like a swear word. He's a black-out drunk with a history of aggressive outbursts."

"There wasn't a bear?" Anika asked. "What about the food all over the ground?"

"I don't know," Dad snapped, then relented. "Sorry. I'm tired. Mom's tired. We want to get home and get some sleep."

The trip out of the valley was faster than the trip in, the switchbacks lifting them up and out of the granite prison. Anika considered giving the middle finger to the ranger standing outside the gatehouse and next to the sign, "Thank you for visiting Yosemite National Park," but he didn't look like he'd had a good sleep either, so she let him off with a warning head shake.

Anika didn't tell her friends she was home. She was supposed to be away until Monday night, so she had some breathing room. She'd wanted to get back to civilization so badly, but when the pod rolled onto the Bay Bridge the distant city looked flat and gray, as if someone had turned down the saturation while she was gone. Scrawny street trees, struggling to survive in tiny three by three-foot holes in the concrete, looked like stunted bushes. Her own backyard, huge by San Francisco standards, felt cramped and hemmed in on all sides by looming buildings.

Mom and Dad unloaded the pod then headed upstairs for a nap.

Anika wandered their compact house in agitation. She was hungry, but when she opened the fridge nothing looked good. She was tired, but when she flopped down on the couch and shut her eyes she saw campfires and waterfalls and turgid rivers. She stank of smoke and sweat, and maybe of Kiaan. She threw off the afghan and headed to the shower.

Water didn't wash away the torrent of emotions. Anxiety that a baby could disappear. Shame that she hadn't helped Mom search. Anger at Yosemite for blocking WorldNet. Relief that nothing had happened to her. Confusion and pride when she remembered that something had—Kiaan—or perhaps more accurately, she'd happened to him.

She dried and dressed in her favorite jeans and a loose black t-shirt, then opened the 3D modeling project for school on her bedroom desk screen, hoping the logic of math would calm her. When the complex bamboo forest finally rendered, the stalks and leaves looked stiff and artificial. How could she have been so proud of this a day ago, and why had she decided to model bamboo? She'd never seen a forest of it in real life, and it wasn't even a California native plant.

She selected the folder holding the work and dragged it to the trash.

Her cuff vibrated. She'd turned it on again once they'd gotten to the Central Valley and familiar chaos swirled across the thousands of tiny screens:

New Episode of Surfline! Join Daniele at Butter Bakery. Anton is an ass. 72 degrees. Anyone want to see the premiere of Flat tonight? 25% off waxing at Pixies. You back yet?

Kiaan—who'd gotten her contact info from their registration card—had sent a couple messages. He apologized for not saying goodbye and wanted to know if she was okay. There was still no clue what happened to the baby. The park wasn't going to turn the jammers back on, so he could keep in touch. So much for what happened in the valley staying in the valley.

The text on her cuff was interspersed with vids of Monica's cat, Jared doing hoverboard tricks on Lombard Street, and sneak previews of the new immersive VR experience on Pier 7.

She'd focused on this bite-sized, digitized, edited, and downsampled version of reality for 17 years and maybe, possibly, probably—it had made her myopic.

She laid her thumb on the cuff to access the preferences menu, scrolled down and down and down until she reached *Release*. Yes, please, she thought, pressing a fingernail into the word. Tiny hasps withdrew, and the cuff fell to the desk.

Her wrist, pale from being covered for so many years, looked thin. She rubbed it. Odd to feel flesh on flesh instead of metal. She waited. Sure enough, 15 minutes later Dad burst through the door, face creased with worry.

"Is something wrong? Your cuff—" He looked from her wrist to the desk.

"I'm not going to wear it anymore."

She'd pushed back on many things—her curfew, not being allowed to go to Oakland warehouse parties, or get a biotattoo—but never the cuff. She expected him to protest, but he merely sighed and sat down heavily on the bed, knocking over Teddy, a stuffed animal she'd had since she was a kid. She tossed it aside to make room for him.

"Is this because of the baby?" he asked.

He wasn't wearing AR glasses. Good. Data would only confuse this issue.

"Not exactly. It's more like…" At moments like this she wished she was better at English than math. "You monitor me to keep me safe." She couldn't help doing air quotes for the last word. "But you can't keep me safe, not really, and I can't make smart decisions if I don't know what's out there. This thing is making me into a moron. All I do is respond to beeps and warnings like a trained animal. I should avoid construction pits because they're huge holes in the ground, not because my cuff tells me to veer right."

She didn't say the rest aloud. *I have no idea what you and Mom consider hazards. What you've been steering me around all these years. People, places, events—what have you hidden from me?* There might be a whole city she'd never seen, just steps from the usual path.

Dad held up his own wrist with a sad smile. "I didn't grow up with this. I don't know who I'd be if my parents monitored me the way we monitor you. I've felt more ambivalent the older you've gotten, but there's pressure from the other parents. From school. If Mom and I said we didn't know where you were or what you were doing…" He laughed. "Well, we'd not be welcome at many of our so-called friend's homes anymore."

He hoisted himself off the bed. "Fuck 'em. You're smart and strong and a good person and I love you. I want to protect you, but you deserve the chance to make mistakes." He hugged her so hard she almost couldn't breathe, then let go and clapped her on the back. "Go get 'em, tiger. I'm going back to bed."

That was it? She'd expected to be grounded, to have her credits line taken away, the battery ripped from her hoverboard. Elation sideswiped her. What now?

She eyed the ill-fitting hiking boots.

Kiaan would be in town next weekend—his parents lived in Berkeley—and he wanted to take her bouldering. She hadn't replied. Yet.

Was "bouldering" a euphemism for another tumble on the mattress? She doubted it. As eager as he'd been in the man cave, he'd been even more excited on stage talking about his real passion. She thought she'd found hers in 3D modeling, but now she wasn't so sure.

What had Kiaan said about bouldering? Nothing but him and the rock…and shoes. She'd need climbing shoes.

SportCenter had a 30-day exchange policy on any product if it was returned in its original packaging. She retrieved the box from the recycling bin, nestled the hiking boots back into the tissue paper, and stowed the box in her backpack.

She crept quietly through the living room so as not to wake her parents, closed the front door slowly so it wouldn't squeak—then hesitated on the porch.

Where the heck was SportCenter? She walked hesitantly down to the sidewalk. She didn't know which direction to head without her cuff and glasses. The unwavering green line her glasses painted had always been her guide. The sidewalk looked empty without it. Although…

She crouched down. Between the broken squares of concrete, delicate moss grew, and amongst the moss, tiny white flowers. She'd never noticed. There wasn't just one green line on the sidewalk, there were many, and they led—

Everywhere.

About the author

M. Luke McDonell's five-minutes-into-the-future fiction explores the effects of emerging technology on individuals and society. Her work has appeared in publications including *Shoreline of Infinity, The Overcast, The Arcanist, Perihelion,* and *New Reader Magazine.*

Her debut novella, *The Perfect Specimen*, was described by one Italian reader as, "Un racconto scritto perfettamente," and is available in print and ebook formats.

By day, she is a senior visual designer and by night she writes and helps run SomaFM internet radio.

Learn more at www.mlukemcdonell.com

www.ingramcontent.com/pod-product-compliance
Lightning Source LLC
Chambersburg PA
CBHW032124050726
47590CB00008B/2950